CINNABAR, THE ONE O'CLOCK FOX

OTHER BOOKS BY MARGUERITE HENRY

Album of Horses
Benjamin West and His Cat Grimalkin
Black Gold
Born to Trot
Brighty of the Grand Canyon
Brown Sunshine of Sawdust Valley
Gaudenzia, Pride of the Palio
Justin Morgan Had a Horse
King of the Wind
Misty of Chincoteague
Misty's Twilight
Mustang, Wild Spirit of the West
San Domingo, the Medicine Hat Stallion
Sea Star, Orphan of Chincoteague
Stormy, Misty's Foal
White Stallion of Lipizza

CINNABAR, THE ONE O'CLOCK FOX

BY MARGUERITE HENRY
Illustrated by WESLEY DENNIS

ALADDIN

NEW YORK LONDON TORONTO SYDNEY NEW DELHI

ALADDIN
An imprint of Simon & Schuster Children's Publishing Division
1230 Avenue of the Americas, New York, NY 10020
This Aladdin paperback edition July 2014
Text copyright © 1956 by Marguerite Henry
Interior illustrations copyright © 1956 by Wesley Dennis
Cover illustration copyright © 2014 by John Rowe
All rights reserved, including the right of reproduction in whole or in part in any form.
ALADDIN is a trademark of Simon & Schuster, Inc., and related logo is a registered trademark of Simon & Schuster, Inc.
For information about special discounts for bulk purchases, please contact Simon & Schuster Special Sales at 1-866-506-1949 or business@simonandschuster.com.
Cover designed by Jeanine Henderson
The text of this book was set in Adobe Garamond Pro.
Manufactured in the United States of America 0315 OFF
10 9 8 7 6 5 4 3 2
Library of Congress Control Number 2014938959
ISBN 978-1-4814-0400-6
ISBN 978-1-4814-0402-0 (eBook)

To L.R. and Emorys

ACKNOWLEDGMENTS

The verses appearing on page 32 are quoted from *Hunting Songs*, by R. E. Egerton-Warburton, published by Constable & Company, London, 1925

The verses on page 124 are adapted from *Scarlet, Blue, and Green*, *A Book of Sporting Verse*, by Duncan Fife, published by Macmillan & Co., Ltd., London, 1932

NO CAGE SHALL HOLD THEM

When this book is published, I shall set free two red foxes who now are living in a big wire-and-wood cage outside my study window. The third cub in the litter was carried all the way to Wesley Dennis's mountaintop in Virginia, where he promptly escaped to freedom in the green, wooded countryside.

But my foxes have been with me since puppyhood. For months now I have studied them by day as they sleep curled up like kittens; and by night as they race pell-mell from one end of the cage to the other, lashing their tails to and fro, and talking some mystic kind of gibberish which is neither like a dog's barking nor a kitten's whimpering. It is their own song to the moon.

These little foxes gingerly take delicacies of chicken livers and beetles right out of my hand; but always their amber eyes gaze at me with an ancient wisdom and dignity, as much as to say: "For now, while we are still cubs, we shall be your pets. But remember, we are creatures of the wildwood, and some night when the moon spills its gold, no cage will hold us." And no cage shall!

I am quick to admit that the fox Cinnabar towers in capabilities above my foxes. But Cinnabar, you see, was never captive. He lived in the time of George Washington, and often—so legend says—he challenged the general to a chase.

Cinnabar represented the spirit of the times, the spirit of a people who fought for freedom and lived for freedom's sake. He eluded all who would catch or trap him, and he finished out his days as a free wild thing.

The word "Cinnabar" comes from the Orient. It means "the red ore of quicksilver." And here is the tale of Cinnabar's adventures when more than once he had a brush with death, but true to his name he slipped away with all the elusiveness of quicksilver.

Wesley Dennis and I have just finished making the pictures and the story come out even; we are still breathless from the chase that Cinnabar has led us. We delight in presenting him to you, and are most grateful to Dorothy Dennis, who first told us of this fearless fox and his hourglass punctuality.

Marguerite Henry

Contents

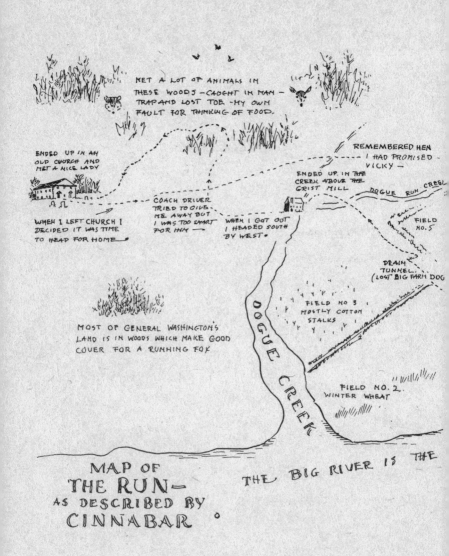

MET A LOT OF ANIMALS IN THESE WOODS — CAUGHT IN MAN — TRAP AND LOST TOE — MY OWN FAULT FOR THINKING OF FOOD.

REMEMBERED HEN I HAD PROMISED VICKY —

ENDED UP IN AN OLD CHURCH AND MET A NICE LADY

ENDED UP IN THE CREEK ABOVE THE GRIST MILL

DOGUE RUN CREEK

COACH DRIVER TRIED TO GIVE ME AWAY BUT I WAS TOO SMART FOR HIM

WHEN I LEFT CHURCH I DECIDED IT WAS TIME TO HEAD FOR HOME

WHEN I GOT OUT I HEADED SOUTH BY WEST

FIELD NO. 5

DRAIN TUNNEL (LOST BIG FARM DOG

FIELD NO 3 MOSTLY COTTON STALKS

MOST OF GENERAL WASHINGTON'S LAND IS IN WOODS WHICH MAKE GOOD COVER FOR A RUNNING FOX

DOGUE CREEK

FIELD NO. 2 WINTER WHEAT

MAP OF THE RUN — AS DESCRIBED BY CINNABAR

THE BIG RIVER IS THE

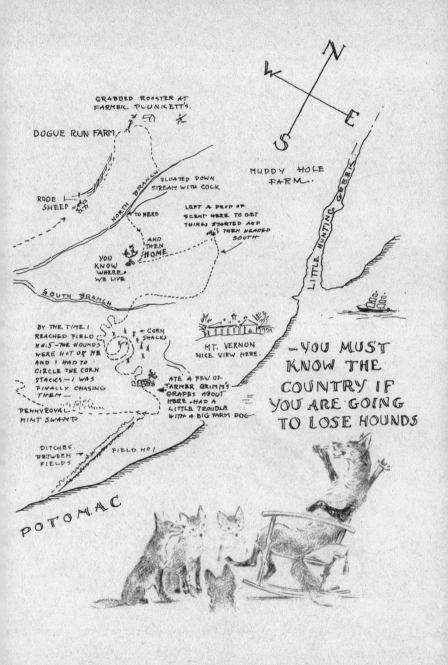

GRABBED ROOSTER AT
FARMER PLUNKETT'S.

DOGUE RUN FARM

N
W   E
S

MUDDY HOLE
FARM.

FLOATED DOWN
STREAM WITH COCK

RODE
SHEEP

TO HERE

LEFT A DROP OF
SCENT HERE TO GET
THINGS STARTED AND
THEN HEADED
SOUTH

AND
THEN
HOME

YOU
KNOW
WHERE
WE LIVE

SOUTH BRANCH

LITTLE HUNTING CREEK

BY THE TIME I
REACHED FIELD
NO.5 — THE HOUNDS
WERE HOT ON ME
AND I HAD TO
CIRCLE THE CORN
STACKS. — I WAS
FINALLY CHASING
THEM —

← CORN
SHACKS

MT. VERNON
NICE VIEW HERE.

— YOU MUST
KNOW THE
COUNTRY IF
YOU ARE GOING
TO LOSE HOUNDS

ATE A FEW OF
FARMER GRIMM'S
GRAPES ABOUT
HERE — HAD A
LITTLE TROUBLE
WITH A BIG FARM DOG

PENNYROYAL
MINT SWAMP

DITCHES.
BETWEEN
FIELDS

FIELD NO 1

POTOMAC

Cinnabar, the One O'Clock Fox

Chapter 1

FOUR IS A JOLLY NICE NUMBER

It was April in Virginia. The brooks and runs on George Washington's estate were overflowing in their hurry to join the big Potomac. Pussy willows along the banks were swollen to plumpness. And everywhere, the woods and meadows were alive with cheeps and chirrings and little feet scampering.

One morning just before the break of dawn, when

the moon was still shining brightly, four little fox cubs were born in a den tucked away in a sassafras thicket.

Cinnabar, their father, had been out all night, hunting. He wanted to bring a nice plump hen to his wife, because she liked nice plump hens. And if ever there was a time to please Vicky, as he called her, it was now. This very night.

Cinnabar's masklike face, with its slanted amber eyes, looked up at the great white face of the moon. But that is not what he saw. He saw instead the warm coziness of his own den. And there was Vicky, still busy at the nestbox weaving a mattress of grasses and reeds. He

knew what that meant. It meant furry little foxes—any moment now.

He bayed his happiness to the moon: *"Yapp yurr. Yapp yur-rrr."* He disappeared into a tangle of honeysuckle and hauled out the fat hen that he had cached away an hour before. Then he pawed deeper into the tanglewood and gathered up four good-sized barn mice. He took them one at a time and placed them side by side neatly and securely underneath the hen's wings.

"My stars and garters!" he barked to himself. "It's been a capital night for hunting!" Grabbing the hen's neck in his mouth, he flung her over his shoulder and trotted off toward home.

Cinnabar was a big, red, magnificent fellow. Courage and heart showed in the very look of him. A rough scar across his nose and a nick on one ear in no way marred his handsomeness. On the contrary, they gave him a gay and gallant air. They spoke of battles won—over eagles and buzzards and hawks and weasels.

Cinnabar was, in truth, afraid of nothing. Neither of dark nor of storm; nor of hunters nor hounds. He was free and unfearing, the very spirit of the wilds.

With a windblown movement he went gliding along, his brush of a tail stretched out full. His lively ears pricked to and fro, catching every sound of the night. Pine needles singing. Frogs playing their bassoons. Birds beginning to stir and twitter. It seemed to him that the morning was coming in with a peculiar gladness.

Silently he left the big trees behind and trotted down a little avenue of hemlocks. Fast as he traveled, his imagination went faster still. He could almost hear Vicky's cry of delight when she spied not only the plump hen, but the four good mice as well. "How she likes hens and mice!" he mused. "Better than grouse and grasshoppers. Better than anything . . . except me!" he chuckled, as he shifted his burden to the other shoulder.

Chatting and laughing and happy in himself, he threaded his way through the sassafras thicket that hid his den. But as he approached the opening, he stopped dead. What were those strange sounds? He thought he heard small trills and whimperings.

"Criminy, criminy, and by Jimminy!" he exploded. "I must be a father. I hear puppy voices. Unmistakably, I do."

Parting the ferns that screened the doorway, he pattered softly through them. Then wriggling forward on his belly, he bunted the hen down the dark entry and finally emerged into the warm comfort of his own den. He blinked his eyes at the brightness. A wick burning in an oyster shell gave off a yellow light, and the fire in the grate was a red glow.

"That you, Cinny?" a voice came muffled.

In reply, Cinnabar barked two short barks and one long. It was the family signal, and it meant "Good hunting tonight." He saw Vicky now—up on one elbow, half sitting, half reclining in the nestbox—and he could hear her tongue strokes, licking, licking, licking.

Little shivers of excitement raced up and down his spine. How many pups would there be this time? Two? Four? Nine? Twelve?

"I shall be quite content with three," he told himself as he took a step closer, "and I hope they all have blue eyes. Blue eyes bewitch me."

Vicky was eager to tell about her babies. She gave four quick, happy barks.

"Oh! Four is a jolly nice number," Cinnabar assured her. "'Twill be easy to provide for them." He laid the big white hen in a splash of firelight, hoping Vicky would notice. But she was concerned only with her young ones.

"My dear," said Cinnabar with a proud grin, "have you thought of names for the funny snub-nosed things?"

"Cinnabar! They are *not* funny snub-nosed things. Oh, yes, they are," she laughed, contradicting herself all in the same breath. "Well, anyway, I've named the two little boys."

"So?" asked Cinnabar, shoving the hen closer.

"Yes. And I do hope you like family names."

"F'rinstance?"

"Rascal for my brother, and Pascal for my father."

"I like them indeed!" Cinnabar nodded in approval as he plucked at his whiskers thoughtfully. Then reaching

into the nestbox he fondled the fuzzy little creatures. "Hmmm—how about Merry and Mischief for the vixens?" he asked, looking all merry and mischievous himself.

Vicky sighed in envy. "How *do* you do it? It took me hours to think up Rascal and Pascal, and you . . . you thought up Merry and Mischief just like that!"

"It was nothing," Cinnabar said modestly. "Nothing at all. I once knew some people by those names."

"And how shall you spell 'Merry?'" Vicky asked, as she settled deeper into the nestbox. "M-a-r-y or M-e-r-r-y?"

"Oh, the latter way! For if she is anything like you, my dear, that would fit her the better. And now if you will tell me where you've put the wild duck eggs, I shall prepare us a breakfast that *is* a breakfast. Meanwhile, you just go on with your licking and nursing."

Vicky gave a sigh of contentment. "The wild duck eggs," she said, "are buried in the sand, down in the cellar."

The den of Cinnabar was as snug and well furnished as one could find in all Virginia. It was sleeping chamber, library, dining room, and kitchen all in one. A round flat stone, fitted onto a stumplike growth, made a nice dinner table, and the seats around it were the twisted roots of a tree. Natural rock made the chimneypiece. And above the mantel hung a gaily decorated map of Cinnabar's hunting territory, while on either side were bookcases stacked with friendly books, bound in birchbark. On the mantel shelf was an hourglass, a three-minute glass, and several quaint pieces of drift that Cinnabar had picked up along the Potomac. An old-time chair set on barrel-stave rockers stood in one corner near the fireplace. And in the other was the nestbox. The only touches of color were the pale green ivy that clambered over the latticed roots of the ceiling, and a sweet potato vine sprouting from a hanging basket.

Cinnabar's eyes roved with pleasure about his home; then they fell upon the hen lying at his feet. He could restrain himself no longer. "My dear!" he exclaimed. "What think you of this white biddy; what think you of her? I caught her amidst the wildest turmoil in Deacon Doolittle's henhouse."

"Oh, Cinnabar, how could you! Deacon Doolittle has been so good to you. Remember the time when you were a young pup and the hounds were after you and he threw his jacket over you and picked you up bodily until they were gone?"

"I do indeed! So I did him a good turn, too. I caught four mice in his corncrib, and here they are!"

Flipping back the hen's wings, he exposed the four fat mice with their gnawing teeth quite visible.

Vicky sat bolt upright. "Cinny, you *are* wonderful. Simply wonderful. You always do more to help the farmer than to hurt him. But I'm not up to preparing a big meal today. Let's have it tomorrow."

Pleased and proud, Cinnabar pulled the hen over to the stairway and pushed her down. "I'll pluck her later," he promised himself.

Breakfast preparations now went on with great slap and dash. Cinnabar never could understand why Vicky made such work of it. He ran gaily down to the cellar and sniffed his way to a small sandbar. Scooping in among the grains of sand, he uncovered two wild duck eggs. Then back up the stairs he went, bounding on his hind legs, and hugging the eggs with his forepaws.

He felt good! The fire was crackling merrily. Vicky was making little snoring noises. And the pups were squirming and suckling.

Humming an old hunting tune, he reached for the skillet hanging beside the mantel. He tossed some goose grease into it, cracked the eggs against the fireplace and plopped them into the pan. The yolks stayed whole, and they were like big bulgy eyes looking up at him. "Funny thing," he winked right back at them, "the rougher you treat eggs, the less apt they are to break; but coddle them, and the yolks squish all over."

"Coddle them!" The thought struck him. Why not? Yes, he would coddle them. Vicky liked them that way. He looked at her tenderly. It must be tiring, having pups. He was glad he was a dog-fox. Hunting was his life. And *being* hunted. He liked danger, excitement, adventure. It made him feel every inch a fox.

The eggs were sending up a delicious fragrance. They were nice and strong and old. "I like my eggs high," he mused as he tossed them up and over and caught them back in the skillet again.

"Pffst! Vicky!" he called. "Wake up and feast upon wild duck eggs. Coddled."

Vicky covered her cubs with a puff of thistledown and came yawning happily across the den. She noticed that the eggs were fried, not coddled, but she was so glad to have someone do the cooking for her that she said not a word.

Cinnabar now slid each egg onto a beech leaf, and next he studied the relish bottles, reading their labels aloud: "Grasshoppers. Red-legged beetles. Crickets." Drooling in delight, he shook some beetles into his paw, crunched them to a fine powder and sprinkled it over the eggs. Then he and Vicky sat down to table.

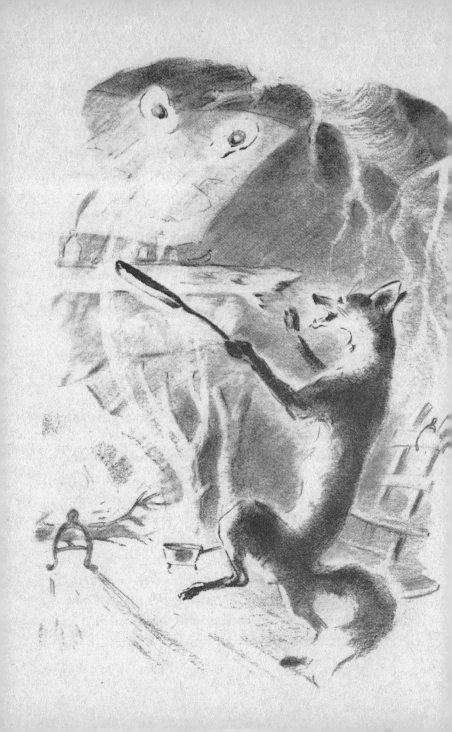

"If you please, Cinnabar, may I have a smidgen more of the beetle seasoning? I love the bittersweet taste and the crunchiness."

Cinnabar burst out laughing. "Remember, my dear, when you refused seasonings and sauces of any kind? What a gourmet you have turned out to be!"

"And all because of you, Cinny. You taught me that a dash of this or that is the difference between a dull meal and a delicious one. Which reminds me . . . would you please to get down that volume of *Unfamiliar Quotations*? I think I can put my paw on the very one I want. And while you are up," she added, "please to bring me my spectacles. In my haste to get into the nestbox, I think I dropped them underneath."

Cinnabar obliged.

"Let me see . . . Let me see." Vicky pawed through the pages and found one marked with a slice of bacon. "Here it is! Listen, my dear." She took a nibble of the bacon; then adjusting her glasses, she read in her lilting voice:

> *"Oh, the little more, and how much it is.*
> *And the little less, and what worlds away."*

Cinnabar stopped lapping the egg yolk and scratched his ear reflectively. "My sentiments exactly. *Exactly!* And it doesn't apply to just sauces and seasonings."

"Of course not."

"It applies to the big things. Like doing everything real good."

"Real well, you mean."

"All right, all right," chuckled Cinnabar. "I mean

putting your heart and soul into things. Whether 'tis hunting or *being* hunted. And I mean doing a jot and a tittle more than is expected of you."

"Oh, Cinny, I love you more each day."

"Pshaw. You just love my cooking," he teased.

Vicky's eyes took on a faraway look. "If only we can bring up our little ones to face life bravely, the way you do."

She put on her glasses once again and eagerly flipped through the pages, talking as she looked. "I don't mean they need to be quite as daring as you, Cinny, so that hunters can count on them exactly at one o'clock. They don't need to be *that* brave . . ." Her voice faded away as she found the passage she was looking for. This time she read only to herself:

> "*Cowards die many times before their deaths;*
> *The valiant never taste of death but once.*"

Silently she repeated the lines, tapping her dainty black foot to emphasize them. "They fit Cinnabar to a T," she thought as she nodded to his resolute words: "We not only *can* teach our cubs to be brave; we *will!*"

Chapter 2

THE CHALLENGE FROM G. WASHINGTON, M.F.H.

With four hungry, begging mouths to be fed, the weeks and months that followed were desperate ones for Cinnabar. He hunted almost to the point of exhaustion. Night after night rains came slanting and slashing down upon the earth. Wildlife holed up. It often took endless hours and every ounce of foxy strategy to catch so much as a mouse. To make matters worse, the storage cellar beneath the den filled up with water, and muddied water climbed up and up the steps until it threatened the den itself.

Meanwhile, Rascal and Pascal, Merry and Mischief were growing beyond belief. They were always hungry, requiring an enormous quantity of bugs and grubs and fish and fowl to keep them full and happy. If Cinnabar was late returning from a night of hunting, they began nibbling at the roots of the dining room chairs. They even stood up on their hind legs and gnawed the books in the shelves.

As summer days came on, Vicky tried to be of help. When her housework was done, she managed to take the children out on mousing and rabbiting trips to give them lessons in scenting and stalking. But hunting was poor that season and they seldom came home with more than a few mealy moths or last year's beechnuts. The burden of the feeding rested heavily on Cinnabar, and as his pups grew stronger and livelier, he grew lean and gaunt, until the crisp autumn days found him but a shadow of his former self.

"What you need, Cinny," Vicky said to him one morning as she was thinning a gruel of acorns, "is a little excitement and fun. All work and no play makes you old before your day."

Cinnabar, at the time, was boning a catfish and tossing morsels first to one yapping mouth and then to another. He looked up in astonishment. How did Vicky know? How could she read his mind? How could she possibly guess that he had a great longing for fun? He yearned to lead the hounds and horses on a merry chase—to tease and trick and baffle them until he could forget, for the moment, that he was weighted down with responsibilities.

Curious, he thought, that Vicky should bring up the matter of fun when it was only yesterday that he had followed a messenger from Mount Vernon who went riding from plantation to plantation. Hidden in the shrubbery, Cinnabar had watched as the man bowed politely at each doorway and presented a white card that he drew from his boot. That card, Cinnabar felt quite certain, was an invitation to the first fall fox chase. For it was exactly the same size as the one he had found last year and hung above his mantel.

As Cinnabar watched unseen, he hoped and prayed that one of the cards would accidentally slip out of the man's boot.

It was almost frightening the way it did! Like something he had willed. Vicky would have called it "spirit magic," for at the third plantation, just as the messenger stepped up on the mounting block, one of the neatly penned cards did slip out from his boot and it fell into a puddle. The man caught sight of the fluttering white

thing, but not wishing to dirty his hands, he left the card where it was. Then he swung into his saddle and took off, singing at the top of his lungs,

"Oh! A-hunt-ing we will go;
A — hunt-ing we will go;
We'll catch the One O'Clock Fox
And put him in a box,
And nev-er let him go."

No sooner had the man's coattails flapped out of sight than Cinnabar boldly trotted from behind a box-wood hedge, pounced on the card, and studied the lines with great hunger and longing in his heart. These were the words he read:

Weather permitting, our first fall fox chase will be held on Saturday next. Gather at Honey Hill at half after ten o'clock. And it was signed G. Washington, M.F.H.

Cinnabar's spirits rose in eager anticipation as he ran home, carrying the card in his teeth. There he threw last year's card into the fire, and with a bit of resin fastened the new one in its place. Then he studied his hunting map, not because he needed to, but as one would study the dear, familiar face of a friend. He knew full well that Honey Hill was only a hoot and a holler from his den. Down the lane between the double row of hemlocks, then over a little footbridge, up a gentle slope, and there you were! Though why they called it Honey Hill, he would never know. Not once had he seen or heard a single honeybee. Oh, well, man's ways were wondrous strange and he was not one to bother his head trying to change things that were. They just were, and that was an end to it.

All these happenings of yesterday flashed through Cinnabar's mind while Vicky was saying, "What you need is a little excitement and fun."

Now he smiled gratefully at her over the heads of their noisy foxlings. A quick shuttle of understanding went almost like a dotted line between them.

"I saw you put up the new card announcing the hunt," Vicky said. "You go, Cinnabar," she added wisely, knowing that he would have to go whether she urged him or not. Regardless of her, regardless of their pups, some things a dog-fox had to do. Things that were expected of him—like being on time to meet a challenge. That card above the mantel said only half. Between the lines they both knew it shouted the words:

COUNT ON THIS: COUNT ON CINNABAR, THE ONE O'CLOCK FOX. SURELY HE WILL BE ON HAND TO GIVE US A GOOD HUNT. ONLY DEATH COULD KEEP HIM AWAY.

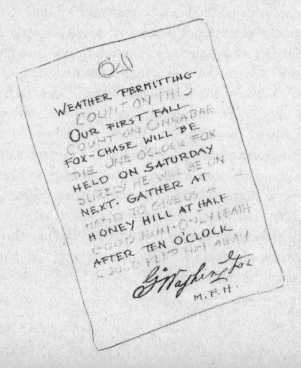

Chapter 3

JUST IN CASE . . .

Saturday dawned in a film of fog. Tangled skeins of mist enveloped trees and bushes as if they were caught up in a cocoon. The dawn found Cinnabar close by his den, dozing in the lee of a fallen log. His brush of a tail still curtained his eyes, letting in only slivers of light. From the *peenk, peenk* of a timberdoodle, he knew, however, that morning had come. Half awake, half asleep, he had the exquisite feeling that today was his. He squinched his eyes and gave his brush a flick and a flirt just to tell himself he was not dreaming; that he was, in fact, Cinnabar, the One O'Clock Fox. And today was his. *For fun.*

With a lusty sigh he rolled over on his back, crossed his paws behind his head, and looked up at the dewy underside of some ferns. A drop of dew splashed right in his eye, and he blinked it away, grinning. He would have to use all his foxy tactics today, for with this moistness his scent would cling sharply to underbrush and grasses.

Fully awake at last, he sat up on his haunches, thinking. Soon the hunters would be jogging to the meet. He saw the whole scene in his mind. The Whippers-In with their long-thonged whips. Billy Lee, the Kennel Huntsman, with his pack of hounds close around him. And there, consulting his watch, would be the Master of the Foxhounds, George Washington. He would be in full regalia of blue frock coat and scarlet vest, both embellished with gold foxhead buttons. And he would be astride Blueskin, his big Irish Hunter. Cinnabar had to laugh to himself. Not only the coat of the horse and of the general looked all of one color, but the braided tail of Blueskin and the pigtail of George Washington looked much alike and stuck out behind at exactly the same jaunty angle.

In his mind's eye, Cinnabar watched the whole field of hunters assemble in the mistiness of the morning.

Then, sighing in animal bliss, he got up, stretching to his full length. He opened wide his jaws and he let his red tongue curl outward until it licked the cool wetness on the fern fronds. He thought with pleasure that he was the center and object of the whole hunt. He had much to do. And now he must stop daydreaming and *do it*.

At a lolloping canter he went down to Dogue Creek, where a sloping bank shelved inward, forming a little hideaway. With his forepaws he dug furiously under the shelf and produced first a gunnysack, all muddy and balled-up, and then a dozen fish heads, which he had banked against just such a day as this. If he should be captured and killed in the hunt, these would keep Vicky and the little ones in food for days to come. He felt good about that.

A crow swooped down low, croaking in his ear and threatening to steal the fish away. But Cinnabar snapped right back at him: "Oh, no! Not today you don't! Not today, you big black Beelzebub! I never felt so strong. If you weren't old and tough, I'd catch you and take you home, too."

"Naw! Naw!" squawked the crow. And off he flew, knowing he was no match for Cinnabar today.

Chapter 4

AND LONG MAY HE LIVE

When Cinnabar arrived at the dooryard of his den, his cubs neither heard nor saw him. They were tumbling and wrestling in the puppy game of romps. He set down his gunnysack of fish heads and stood there a moment, hidden by the ferns. His heart swelled with pride. Rascal, biggest and boldest of the litter, was dancing in circles about Pascal and shaking a wishbone in his mouth. "You can't catch me! You can't catch me!" he teased and taunted.

Merry and Mischief capered about their litter brothers, bouncing on their dainty paws, trying to get into the game.

Cinnabar's eyes sparkled. There was nothing mangy about *his* pups. His were fat and woolly, their bodies strong and agile. "They've had only the best," he thought. Then he had to laugh at himself, for he knew he was really saying that he'd been such a good, faithful, dependable provider that he deserved a day off.

Vicky's head now poked out of the den. "Rascal! Pascal! Merry! Mischief! Your father will be here any moment. Come in at once and wash your paws!"

Instantly the four young foxes dived into their den, and Cinnabar after them.

The washbasin, an ancient trough hollowed out from a log, was now the scene of a lively splash party.

"Vicky!" Cinnabar called above the uproar. "I am in ecstasy."

Vicky smiled indulgently as she cuffed Pascal into position and poured an extra gourdful of water into the trough. "About today's hunt?" she asked.

"Aye! Aye!" Cinnabar sighed happily. "Curds and whey, what a day! The air is dripping with moisture and my scent will cling primely to brush and briar and stalk and stubble. Oh, curds and whey, what a day!"

For sheer joy he picked up the nearest cub, which

happened to be Merry, and tossed her high into the air. He watched her land with elfin grace, and again his heart expanded with pride.

"Vicky, Vicky, Vicky," he laughed, "should the hounds tear me to pieces today, be not one whit sorry."

"Cinn-a-*bar*!" Vicky's voice held terror in it. "I will *not* have you talking like that in front of the children."

"Tush, tush, my dear, they are so busy playing wetpaw that we scarce exist. Except," he added with a

twinkle, "at hungry-time. Which reminds me . . ."

"Of what, Cinnabar?"

The cubs now came bouncing about their father, waving their brushes from side to side in expectancy. "What did you bring us, Papa Cinny?"

"Fish heads—for tomorrow and tomorrow," replied Cinnabar. Then he slung the gunnysack over his shoulder and disappeared into the cellar, where he covered each fish head carefully with sand, tamping it down with his nose.

When he returned, the den was in apple-pie order. The children were all seated, their forepaws crossed and resting lightly on the edge of the table. They looked half angel, half fox.

"What's this? What's this?" exclaimed Cinnabar. "Such a lovely silence I hear. Vicky, were *we* ever that quiet as pups?"

Vicky made no answer. Her eyes were bright with the little surprise she had planned. From the mantel she now took a box, opened the lid, and held up an heirloom that had come from her side of the family. It was a twin flute, so highly polished that it gleamed in the firelight. Gracefully she lifted it to her muzzle and with a light breath sounded an "A."

Four little urchin faces tossed upward as if they were on one stalk, and four small squeaky voices answered the "A."

Then with Vicky's foot tapping out the rhythm, a rollicking sound burst forth until the words and tune made the den ring:

"Few sportsmen so gallant, if any,
Did cubs ever send to the chase;
Each dingle for him has a cranny,
Each river a fordable place.

"He knows the best line from each cover,
He knows where to stand for a start,
And long may he live to fly over
The country he loves in his heart."

For a long moment Cinnabar stood upright on his hind legs. He was speechless. He looked on them all, on Rascal and Pascal and Merry and Mischief, and thence a sidelong glance at Vicky, who was wiping the flute on her apron. Not a sound escaped him. Not even a sigh. Then, still on his hind legs, he tittuped softly about the den, doing a sailor's hornpipe dance.

At last he found his voice.

"Bravo! Bravo!" he shouted so loudly that a pebble bounced from the chimneypiece and landed plumb in Mischief's lap.

This sent everyone into peals of laughter. But Cinnabar's laughter was cut short. His eye was drawn to the passageway that led to the out-of-doors. His thoughts began to race. "My stars! The slanting morning's sun is gone. It must be high noon. I have only an hour to meet the hunt, only an hour to ready myself!"

Vicky followed his glance and turned the hourglass

An old, old hunting song

Music by Russell Jupp

Few sports—men so gal—lant if an——y did cubs ev—er send to the chase; each dingle for him has a cran——ny, each riv—er a ford—a—ble place. He knows the best line from each co—ver, He knows where to stand for a start, And long may he live to fly o—ver the coun—try he loves in his heart.

so the sands would trickle the moments away. Then she busied herself sampling the pheasant consommé that was simmering over the fire. It needed more seasoning, and she set the children to chipping crystals of salt from a salt block.

Cinnabar, meanwhile, took a comb made of chicken ribs and proceeded to groom his brush from the very root to the white tag at the tip. Excitement made his paws tremble.

Vicky was quick to notice. "Here, Cinnabar, I'll put

your bowl of soup on the table. Take a little sippet now and again, as you make ready. It will steady your nerves. Nothing better for the nerves than hot consommé with celery root; that's what your granny, old Madame Bushy, used to say." Vicky put the steaming bowl on the table and placed four smaller ones in front of Rascal, Pascal, Merry, and Mischief.

For once the cubs were too spellbound to eat. They were fascinated with what they saw and heard *and smelled*. Not only was Cinnabar combing each hair separately, but he was dipping his comb into a pinch bottle marked "Skunk No. 5." To the cubs it was the most teasing, tantalizing, sweet, musky fragrance they had ever sampled.

Rascal snuffed noisily. "Comb me, too, Papa! Please! Please!" he begged.

"Comb me!"

"Comb me!"

"Comb me!" echoed the other cubs.

"Shush!" commanded their mother. "Your father is a busy fox. Lap up your soup at once before it gets cold." She turned now to her husband, and a shyness crept into her voice. "Cinnabar," she hesitated, "I've another surprise. I sent to Tattersall's in London and had them order for you a scarlet vest complete with golden buttons and lace to match George Washington's. I *had* planned to give it to you for Christmas, but as I stirred your consommé, the pieces of celery formed many letters of the alphabet, and bless my soul if they didn't make a little sentence."

"Bumpkins and pumpkins!" Cinnabar exclaimed incredulously. "And what did the letters say, my dear?"

"They repeated the motto on your family coat of arms. The Latin for 'Do it now! Do it now!'" And suiting her action to the motto, Vicky produced a splendid vest from a box marked "Tattersall's of London."

Cinnabar looked up from his combing to see a beautiful replica of the enemy's foxhunting apparel. The vest was, in every detail, identical to that worn by the Master of Foxhounds, George Washington. Even to the hunt buttons with grinning fox faces.

"Slip into it, Cinny. It will keep you warm on a misty, moisty day like this. Let's see the fit of it."

Cinnabar began hedging for time. Could he accept the costume of his mortal enemy? Besides, any vest at all would be a hindrance, not a help. In fording streams it would get wet and soggy. As for the color, it would shout his whereabouts whenever he wanted to hide. But he dare not hurt Vicky's feelings. He must be tactful and foxy and kind. Suddenly a thought struck him. As he slipped it on, he let all the air out of his lungs and pulled in his belly, making himself as thin as possible.

"Oh, oh, *oh*!" wailed Vicky. "It's too big! Much, much too big! It won't do at all. I won't *let* you wear it."

Cinnabar shook his head sadly and put his free paw, the one without the comb in it, around Vicky. "Don't feel bad, my pet. Being remembered is what matters. The gift is fine. Superfine! And soon Rascal or Pascal will grow into it."

Time was running out. Each half of the hourglass showed the same amount of sand.

Cinnabar corked the bottle of Skunk No. 5 and laid his comb on the mantel. He surveyed himself in a treasured piece of looking glass that he had retrieved from George Washington's trash pile. "And now, dear lady, would you say that I look all bright-eyed and bushy-tailed?"

"I would indeed!" Vicky nodded as she put the remains of the soup, with all the celery root, into his bowl. "Now lick up!" she urged. "I don't like to have you go out on an empty stomach."

Cinnabar sat down to the table, lapping the delicious consommé slowly, thoughtfully.

"Frightened, Cinny?" asked Vicky.

"No, of course not," chuckled Cinnabar. "The joy of the chase is greater by far than the fear of the hounds."

Now he cleared his throat and pointed to the hourglass. "Time is fleeting," he said in a voice vibrant with anticipation for the fun and danger to come.

Chapter 5

I SHALL LEAVE MY SCENT WHERE THE
CATTAILS GROW

The den suddenly went silent. All eyes were on the
hourglass. Even the cubs stopped eating and watched
with an awareness beyond their tender age.

Trickle . . . trickle . . . trickle went the last little grains
of sand. Now the bottom of the bell-shaped glass held
them all. The top was nothing but emptiness, except for
a fine film of dust where the sand had been.

"One o'clock!" Cinnabar's voice boomed. Then he gulped the last bit of soup, frisked his paw through his whiskers, and looked from one to the other. "I bid you all adieu," he said with a grand flourish.

"Oh!" pleaded Vicky, "try to be careful! Did you know," she added in concern, "that George Washington has some new, extra-fast foxhounds?"

"Of course I know!" laughed Cinnabar. "'Twas myself who told you. General Lafayette sent them all the way over the seas from France. The leader, I hear, is a young lady hound named Sweet Lips because her baying is so high and sweet it makes your very blood tingle."

"And *I* hear those 'Sweet Lips' hide fangs of death. They can crunch a fox's leg as if it were a carrot. Oh, Cinny, don't go! Please don't go. Any other fox would hole up in his den on a day like this."

Cinnabar was now rolling on the grass doormat to

give his coat an extra sheen. "Your mother," he winked at the cubs as he rolled back and forth, "says one thing with *her* sweet lips, and quite another thing with her eyes. What her eyes say is: 'Get going, Cinnabar! Take life in your teeth, and if you're going to go, *go*!'"

Saying which, he leaped lightly to his feet, gave each of his children a loving spank, and headed for the door.

"Cinny!" Vicky stopped him with her voice. "If you have a moment during the chase, grab off one of Mister Plunkett's hens. They're fat as butter, and I've a craving for a good, fat hen. Besides, he's careless about his fences and this may teach him a lesson."

"Consider it done, my dear," Cinnabar called back over his shoulder. "You have the currant jelly ready; I'll bring the hen. I shall be home by starlight, I don't doubt."

Like a puff of smoke, swiftly, noiselessly, Cinnabar glided up the tunnel and out into the glimmering world of sun and shadow. He lifted his face to the wind and snuffed the invigorating smells from the woods nearby—rabbits, quail, wild turkeys. He drew a great lungful of the wonderful mixture.

The morning's mist had lifted, and a gossamer radiance filtered through the wispy clouds. An exquisite sense of liberty made his whole body quiver. He was a free fox; a wild fox. He felt as young as one of his own cubs. Joyously, he slipped through the sassafras thicket, then down the little lane between the hemlocks, and up the winding path to a knoll overlooking the whole of George Washington's hunting grounds. From this lofty perch he scanned the distance, surveying the ups and downs of the land. What he saw was rolling hills and deep valleys, and winding creeks glinting from the touch of sun. He saw farmland and meadow, and far off the white mansion house with

its cluster of little buildings, like chicks sidling up to a mother hen. But mostly he saw woodland with pine trees growing, and he heard the steady whisper of wind in the treetops.

With his head cocked a little to one side, he turned now to look at the small shadow he made. His heart began to beat faster. It was just past the hour of one. The hunters must surely be headed his way by now. But which covert would they draw? Which line would they take? He stood up, pricking his ears, then swiveling them like a man with an ear trumpet. Although the sharpest human ears could scarcely have heard so faint a sound,

Cinnabar's caught a single high note. The Huntsman's horn! "Your life is at stake," it said. "The chase is on. *Run,* Cinnabar! *Run!*"

Now he knew which way the hunters were coming. They were directly east of him, in the woods across the creek. The horses would have to ford it, the hounds would have to swim it; then they would come crashing into his own woods and the fun would begin.

Excitement rose in him. He licked his right forepaw and held it up to see which way the wind was blowing. "Hmmm," he breathed. "'Tis a west wind. I shall skally-hoot down to the edge of the creek, and there I shall

leave a spot of scent where the cattails grow. And West Wind shall blow my scent in the hounds' faces. I *want* them to chase me!"

He waited until the very last moment, waited until he heard the cracked voice of the Huntsman, crying, "Yhou-whou-whou," encouraging the hounds, telling them to enter the creek.

Then, with a swift, winnowing movement, he headed downhill, brushed against the cattails to leave his scent, and returned again to the little knoll to wait.

For an awesome moment the world was wrapped in silence, except for a lone bird singing in a wild persimmon tree.

All of a sudden the quiet exploded. Horses and hounds came splashing across the creek, and the pack fanned out along the bank, thrashing in and out among the scrub willow and honeysuckle. It was Sweet Lips who first caught a tiny drift of oily, musky fragrance. She began working the scent, sifting it from the smell of beavers and muskrats. She yipped a little, not quite certain at first. Then she doubled back again to check, and now she was sure! With a long-drawn howl she spoke out. Hounds and men, and even Cinnabar, knew the cry. "I'm on the line!" it said. "I've scented a fox!"

"Hark to her! Hark!" the Huntsman's voice bellowed.

From all over the bank the hounds came in to Sweet Lips. One by one they too picked up the trail and gave tongue until the medley of their voices spread like a wave. The woods caught up the sound and tossed it back and forth from tree to tree.

Cinnabar's heart thumped wildly. At last! At last they were coming for him! The crash of hound music touched off a fuse inside him. It was as if all of life had been building up to this moment.

"Oh, frogs and mice, and all things nice!" he trilled in rapture. Then up he sprang into the air, flaunting his tawny red coat against the blue of sky. And so, in full view of thirty eager horsemen and a pack of bloodthirsty hounds, he went flying downhill. Bravely, he headed toward them, then with a teasing grin, he circled in front of them and veered away like a wisp of red vapor.

"TALLY HO"

Chapter 6

SWEET LIPS IS OUTFOXED

T al-ly Ho!" It was George Washington who sighted the flying form of Cinnabar. "Tal-ly ho!" he cried, standing up in his stirrups and pointing his cap in Cinnabar's direction. "'Tis the One O'Clock Fox!"

"Tal-ly ho! Tal-ly ho!" echoed the Whippers-In, while Billy Lee lifted his big brass horn to heaven and played a joyous spirtle of notes. "Gone a-way! Gone a-way!" the notes said.

Within a hundred yards of the oncoming pack,

Cinnabar stopped an instant to plan his route. The map in his mind suddenly came clear. To the south lay Union Farm, Field Number Four. Yes! He would take it! Time enough later to twist and turn, and needle in and out of hedgerows. Now he was fresh and strong. Yes! To the green field of winter wheat. Cinnabar, the One O'Clock Fox, would give them a run to remember.

With the pack yelping in pursuit, he laid back his ears and straightened away. The hounds went hard from the start. Theirs was the advantage. Wind in their faces. Scent heavy and pungent. The wheatfield new-green and smooth.

In a diagonal line Cinnabar flew. He loved the rush of the run with a wild and passionate love. There was nothing to stop him. Acres and acres lay stretched out before him. It was as if Vicky had unfurled a green carpet and had called out, "Here, Cinny, run! Run, run, *run*!"

Behind, he could hear the hounds baying and the horses making thunder with their hoofs. His lope became a gallop. Run, run! Run for the pure joy of running. Suck in fresh air. Hind legs leap ahead of forelegs. Skim the earth. Go! Go! Go! Eat up the green mile. A hundred yards, two hundred yards. Three hundred. Suck in more breath. Let your tongue whip out of your mouth, a bright red streamer. Flush a covey of quail. Skitter and squawk them up to the sky. Go! Go! *Go!*

Soft and velvety, the wheatfield stretches on. How good it feels! Keep going, Cinnabar! Keep going! No hollow trees to hide in. Not even a rabbit's nest. Run, run, *run*!

The Huntsman's voice closer. "For'ard, Sweet Lips and Chanter! For'ard, June and Jowler! For'ard, Rhapsody, good fellow!"

The hounds now gaining. The horses gaining. Cinnabar *had* to widen the gap. He *had* to catch his breath. The wind dried his tongue until he could scarce swallow. And just when the hounds were close on him, the map in his mind said, "Yonder it is! Yonder the ditch that marks the edge of the field. Run for it! Run, Cinnabar, run!"

In a wild spurt he reached the yawning ditch, and with a single leap disappeared into it. What's this? What's this? A deserted fox den right here? With a nick

and a turn he was inside its cobwebby darkness while the pack of hounds and the whole field of hunters jumped over his head.

"Oh, beetles and bugs, what fun!" he panted as he lay there on his belly.

One minute to rest. Two minutes. Three. Precious time to rest. Time to breathe, and time to chuckle, too. For Sweet Lips had lost the first skirmish. Her high bugling was fading off to silence.

Cinnabar laughed, laughed aloud. "Oh, my brush and whiskers! Wouldn't Vicky and the cubs love to be hiding in here with me!" He began humming to himself as he swept the cobwebs from his nose:

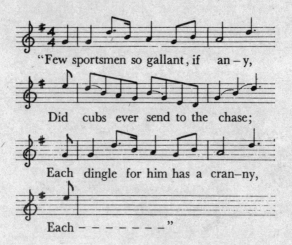

"Few sportsmen so gallant, if an-y,
Did cubs ever send to the chase;
Each dingle for him has a cran-ny,
Each – – – – – – –"

Crash! Sweet Lips had fanned back on the line. Her tonguing came fiercer, faster, louder. The other hounds joined her, uproarious as they, too, struck the scent again.

Quick, Cinnabar, what now? They'll find your hiding place. Sniff about the den. Is there a hidden exit? Probe with your nose. Here. There. Everywhere.

Eureka! The wall gives way to his bunting. Another tunnel, a winding run, half closed by fallen earth. Fiercely he paws the dirt away, then wriggles through the opening until once more he is peering out at the big wide world.

For a moment the light blinded him. But almost in his ears he heard the Huntsman's horn playing a string of choppy notes:

"Ta, *ta* . . . Ta, *ta* . . . Ta, *ta* . . . Ta, *ta* . . . Ta, *ta* . . . Ta, *ta* . . . Ta, *ta* . . ."

"Come in!" the notes said. "The fox must have turned here!"

Quickly Cinnabar scampered along the ditch until he came to a place where the willows made umbrellas of their branches. There, hidden from view, he sneaked up and over the bank, then dashed across the grazing meadow that bordered Dogue Run. With a soaring leap he sailed over the water, swished through the tall grass on the far side, and stole into the shocks of corn in Field Number Five.

"I may lose 'em in this dry field," he thought. "My scent won't hold here."

Chapter 7

TURNABOUT!

Field Number Five was e-*nor*-mous! Ever so much larger than the wheatfield. All around, as far as the eye could see, there were standing shocks of Indian corn, like little brown wigwams. And between them, fat-bellied pumpkins ripening in the sun.

Cinnabar sighed in relief as he wound in and out among the shocks at an easy pace. How he loved life and living! "But," he told himself, "being game and plucky is one thing; being a foolish knothead is quite another.

From now on I'd better keep more distance between me and the hounds."

Glancing back, Cinnabar could not even see them. They were working up and down the rows tediously, so faint was the scent. He could hear their occasional yapping as they unraveled his winding trail.

Nimbly he made great sweeping "S's" around the shocks, letting his body fall into a pleasant swaying rhythm. What a holiday this was! Flowing along, drifting along, free as air. He tasted the scent of rabbits in the busy whisper of wind, but he did not stop to investigate. Today he was the hunted, not the hunter. He seemed one with the wind, a streamer of wind himself.

A flock of wild pigeons rose in front of him with a whizzing and whirring of wings. The dust they raised made him sneeze and cough.

"I wish I had something cool to drink," he thought.

"Not icy cold like spring water, but just cool enough to slake my thirst."

A happy idea came to him. Wouldn't a juicy grape taste good? If he headed for the lower end of the field, he would come upon the kitchen gardens of Union Farm, and there would be the old stone wall covered with big clusters of glossy black grapes.

Still holding a winding course, he aimed for the gardens and the delicious grapes. Already in his mind's eye he could see them spilling over the wall. Already they tickled his tongue with their juiciness. He could hardly wait! He pushed on, keeping a measured distance before the hounds. And then, almost there, an angry growl came at him, not from behind, but from the direction of the wall! It was the low snarl of a watchdog.

A hoarse voice belonging to Farmer Grimm cried out, "Sic 'im, Ripper! Sic 'im! Whomsoever it is, sic 'im!"

Cinnabar halted, tense and still. The taste of dog came sharp to his nostrils. Now only a few yards ahead he saw a huge mongrel coming at him, jaws snapping, white fangs gleaming. And behind he heard Sweet Lips and the pack baying on the line.

Danger ahead! Danger behind! What should he do?

He began muttering excitedly to himself. "If I dive into the center of the field and pull the whole hunt in after me and then loop around the shocks in great big circles, soon I'll be chasing them!" He veered off at a tangent and began weaving in and out of the shocks in a

circle, an ever-widening circle until . . . "Bless my bushy tail!" he barked. "The tables are turned!"

They were indeed. Cinnabar was coming up behind the field of horsemen and the milling pack. Now *he* was chasing the hunt, and they were chasing the big mongrel, who had come to join the fun.

"Oh, bows and arrows, titmice and sparrows!" he whistled, as the field became a whirling mass of flap-eared hounds and galloping horses. "It's just as I planned!"

Farmer Grimm added to the confusion, bellowing

at his dog and flailing the air with his fists. Suddenly he stopped in openmouthed wonder as Cinnabar cut out of the circle, ran around behind the farmhouse, and dashed for the kitchen gardens. There he leaped up onto the stone wall and came to rest like a fox in a fable.

The farmer followed, huffing and puffing and shouting his threats. "I'll git ye, ye red demon, for stealin' my grapes!"

Quite nonchalantly Cinnabar was plucking the biggest ones and crunching them with his fine white teeth. He was even spitting out the skins and savoring the juicy pulp, as if he owned the whole of Union Farm!

This was too much for Farmer Grimm. "General!" His voice came loud as a war whoop. "General Washington!" he bawled above the cries of the hounds. "Here! Here on the wall is your sassy varmint!"

Chapter 8

A MINTY DISGUISE

Feeling smug and happy and full of glee, Cinnabar continued to sit upon the wall eating grapes. He listened to the yammering of the hounds as they chased the Ripper, and to the anxious Huntsman calling the pack. "Leu in! For'ard, Sweet Lips and Chanter! For'ard, June and Jowler! For'ard, Rhapsody, good fellow! Leu in, Meadow Lark!"

Above the uproar came the piercing voice of Farmer Grimm. "Ripper! You addlepated cur! Chase the *fox*!"

Cinnabar parted the vines and looked out. The Ripper was seemingly deaf. He was dogging Sweet Lips's steps, ignoring his master as something small and distant and unimportant now.

"*You* . . . !" Farmer Grimm swung around, venting his wrath on Cinnabar. "You red varmint, *you*! If'n you cause me to lose my dog to the pack, I'll catch ye in a trap and I'll skin ye alive!"

Cinnabar grinned in the man's face. "Sticks and stones may break my bones," he barked, "but words will never hurt me." Then, snatching a last grape, he leaped from the high wall across a footpath, and landed on a lower wall that hemmed in the kitchen garden.

Bedlam broke loose. Half of the pack came babbling after him in confusion, trying to pick up the scent. The other half was still after the Ripper, driving him into the potato patch, rolling him atop the piles of sorted potatoes, mixing the large with the small, and the small with the culls.

Farmer Grimm, who had just finished his sorting, jumped up and down in a rage. "Gener-al! Gener-al!" he yelled with all the force of his lungs. "Please to call off yer hounds. Please to call 'em off!"

The general's face turned as scarlet as his vest. He wrenched his horse around. "No! You get that nosy cur of yours out of our pack!" he commanded.

Angrily, Grimm stomped toward the hounds, first yelling at his dog, then wheedling him with a sugary voice. Even the Whippers-In tried to help. They cracked their long-thonged whips to distract the hounds.

If the noise was fearsome before, it was earsplitting now. The hounds were hysterical! Cinnabar's maneuvers were driving them crazy. Always he was on the *other* side. When they were in the vegetable patch, their jaws almost latching on to his brush, he would slither free and with a mighty leap land back on the wall where the grapevine grew. Back and forth, back and forth he jumped, and always he was safe on the other side!

The farmer, now coming up with a club, threw it straight at Cinnabar, who lost his balance and fell off the wall. Like quicksilver he bolted through the hound pack, through the patch of potatoes, through the cabbage patch, through the turnip patch, and then lightly as a cat he landed in the bed of pennyroyal mint. There he rolled and rolled to take on the minty smell and to lose his own musky fragrance. With this disguise he dived into a drain at the edge of the garden.

"Outfoxed!" Farmer Grimm spat the word. "I been outfoxed once too often! *I* got foxy tactics too! I'll go into the woods with my traps, and I'll bait 'em with big snacks of smelly fish. And I'll git him yet!"

Cinnabar, meanwhile, lay sprawled all safe and secure in the drain. "Ho, ho!" and "Ha, ha, ha!" he chortled deep down inside him. He could hardly keep from laughing aloud as he watched a curious parade passing the tiny porthole of his hiding place—a parade of twitching noses, floppy ears, and padded feet. "Wait till Vicky hears about this! Ho, ho . . . ha, ha, ha!"

Chapter 9

A FOX IN A FIX

Watching, not moving, Cinnabar kept himself hidden in the drain. He fancied he saw the big paws of Sweet Lips potter by. Then he saw four paws bigger still. And suddenly a monstrous dog face with little pig eyes thrust itself into the opening.

The Ripper!

At once Cinnabar leaped forward and bit him on the nose.

"Ki-yi!" yelped the big dog. "Ki-yi-i-i-i!" His startled

cries brought the hounds pell-mell. They began pack-ing in around the entrance of the drain, while Cinnabar slyly backed out the other end. All that the hounds smelled was pennyroyal mint, and all that they saw was the Ripper streaking for home, tail between his legs.

Cinnabar took one glance at the pack milling about in confusion. "Now's my chance to dash away free," he thought as he fled to the shelter of a hedgerow. There in the honeysuckle he laid his plans.

Two choices were open to him. He could back-track at once for home, or he could carry on the game. Impulsively he favored more sport. Today was his hard-earned holiday after months of desperate hunting. He had yearned so long for this day, so very long, that he wanted to make it last. He needed a little more fun, just a little more. Then dark would come on and he would be content to go home.

His mind was made up. Fun it would be! He was only a tawny shadow as he crept through the honey-suckle, but the sharp eye of Billy Lee sighted the white tip of his brush, and once again an insistent tootling filled the air: "Ta, *ta* . . . Ta, *ta* . . . Ta, *ta* . . . Ta, *ta* . . . Ta, *ta* . . . Ta, *ta* . . ."

Again the chase was on! Again the hound music as Cinnabar dashed headlong through the bramble, and out upon a field of cotton that sloped away to the creek. Here the soil was red clay, so that Cinnabar was red on red, and he seemed no more than a whisper of movement. Joyfully he dug his toes into the earth, glad to be out of the dark drain, glad to be flying again.

Straight on came the hounds, crashing through the twiggy cotton as fast as their legs could carry them. And behind them the long string of horses.

"Head him! Head him!" It was George Washington calling to the Whippers-In, telling them to steer the fox away from the creek.

But as easily turn back the wind! Dogue Run was Cinnabar's goal! With sublime sureness he fled straight toward the shining stream, while hound voices rang

out full and eager for the kill. Down sloped the land—down, down, down. As he ran, Cinnabar's mind flew on ahead. He could see himself swimming, faster than a beaver, faster than a fish!

It was midafternoon now and the sun was spilling its gold slantwise across the earth. It fired the water into a ribbon of gold, and it made tiny rainbows of the splashing spray against the larger rocks. The shimmering stream, so near and yet so far, dazzled Cinnabar, winking up at him like something alive. "Come to me!" it laughed. "Come to me!"

Glancing back, Cinnabar was shocked to see how the hounds had gained. They were running close packed, their tongues slavering, their voices shrill. He had to reach the creek at once.

Ahead, there it was, snaking along with the shine of gold on its back and the voice of it still laughing up at him. "Come to me! Come to me!"

Frantically he thrashed through the willows, skidded down the slippery bank, and now the cold water was washing up his legs. He couldn't touch bottom! The current swirled him about and lined him downstream. With his nose up and his forepaws paddling like small water wheels, he was rapidly leaving the hunt behind. He looked around and saw that the hounds had stopped at the creek's edge. They were lapping the cold water greedily.

An impish grin crossed his face. "They've had a pretty good run," he laughed. "And now they're drinking their bellies full; that'll slow 'em down."

These thoughts were suddenly dashed out of his head, for the current was growing stronger, swifter. It took command of him. In all his life Cinnabar had never been tossed about like this. He barely managed to suck in a lungful of air, for the rush of water tumbled him along, slapping him this way and that way, cuffing him over the head with pieces of drift.

"Oh, bless my stars!" he gulped in panic. "What shall I do? What *shall* I do?"

"You'll do as I tell you!" the creek spumed in his face, as it rudely shunted him into a narrow wooden flume. It was the raceway to a mill!

With all his might Cinnabar struggled to claw up the slippery sides. But the fast-flowing current said, "No! I've got you in my clutches. I won't let you go!"

In vain Cinnabar fought, fought to leap clear, but the watery ogre drew him under and shot him violently through the race-gate and up against the big mill wheel. Winded, he fell limply onto a moving paddle, with falling water pouring down on all sides.

"Oh, mercy me!" he sobbed. "I'm in a box of water! Help, help! I'm drowning!"

In that frightful moment the paddle began dipping at a crazy angle; then as the wheel continued to turn, Cinnabar was suddenly plummeted into space and dropped into a shallow black pool where there seemed to be no current at all.

There he stood, belly deep, under the shower that splashed down from the wheel. He was a pitiable fellow, waterlogged, bewildered, and utterly spent, coughing, wheezing, and fighting for air.

"Oh, black night!" he gasped. He was in the very bowels of the mill, with dank darkness all around. Only the barest sliver of light showed far above his head. He tried leaping toward it, tried again and again, but it was much too high and far away.

Then in his darkness the words of Grandma Bushy came to him. Wistfully he saw her now, cutting out little cookies in the shape of mice and rabbits and pheasants, and he could hear her lovely voice saying, "Cinny-boy, remember always *every ingress has an egress.*"

Now he thought he knew what she meant. But was it true?

As his eyes became accustomed to the gloom, they were like cat's eyes glowing, and they saw with catlike clearness. Something beside him was moving! It was the big water wheel, the very one that had pitched him down into the dungeon. But now the paddles were traveling upward through that slit in the ceiling. Here was the *egress*!

"Oh, thank you, Grandma Bushy!" Cinnabar piped. "I'll ride a paddle to escape. . . . Surely I can leap that far!"

He tried and failed. With an agonized cry he slipped from the slimy moss-covered paddle, back into the pool. He took a long breather, letting the water wash gently against his legs as it moved slowly toward the tail pond. Then valiantly he tried again. This time his elbows caught the raised edge of a paddle, and his toenails fairly dug into its leached surface. And so he clung for dear life.

"I made it, Grandma Bushy!" he cried. "I made it!"

Yes! The paddle was carrying him up, up, up to the light. He laughed nervously, so great was his relief. "Oh, me! Oh, me!" he kept repeating. "Being caught in the raceway and getting soused was more sport than I bargained for. But I'm not sorry. I'll know better than to enter the creek near the mill again."

In the few seconds as he rose, so did his spirits. His breath came more easily and he rested while the wheel carried him onward. Surely it would end in the great out-of-doors, in a treetop perhaps, and he would scamper down the trunk and hightail it for home.

"Whee!" he shouted and laughed. Like a child on a Ferris wheel he was enjoying his ride to the full when to his surprise he found himself, not outdoors, as he had hoped, but at the first floor of the mill.

A booming voice was saying, "Aye, traveler, the general divides his flour into superfine, fine, middlings, and shipstuff."

Only by the merest chance the miller happened to look up. "Great Jumping Jehoshaphat!" he whistled as he caught sight of Cinnabar atop a paddle. Soon, very soon the little fox would tumble down again, through the water chute and into the dark dungeon. Seeing the danger, the miller cried out, "Here's a fox in a fix!"

With a quick reach he grabbed Cinnabar by the tail and tossed him to safety.

As Cinnabar landed on the floor, he uttered a string of throaty barks. *"Yapp, yurr. Yapp, yapp, yurrrrr."* It was the voice of a wild thing, brave and unafraid. "Think you," it said, "that I would tumble down that chute again? Not me. Not me! Not on your lefe, lofe, life!"

"I'll be hog-switched!" grunted the traveling peddler. He and the miller stared agape as the little fox showered them both with spray from his coat and then went scurrying among the barrels, trying to find a way out. As if his nose were a divining rod, Cinnabar snuffed along the floorboards and drove out of hiding a nervous mother rat with a little train of youngsters. She went skittering around the wooden beams and braces, her family after her.

The miller held his sides in laughter. "This be the craziest fox I ever see," he guffawed as Cinnabar chased the whole family of rats back into their nest. Quite easily he might have caught the last squeaking fellow, which would have made a tasty tidbit, had not the sound of the Huntsman's horn pierced the millhouse.

The miller became a changed man. Grabbing a twig broom, he ran after Cinnabar. "*You* must be the general's quarry!" he gasped as if recognizing a famous character. "Why, you mought be the One O'Clock Fox!" And

brandishing the broom, he yelled to the peddler, "Open that door—the one to the road!"

"Git, you!" shrieked the peddler, kicking at the fox with his boot.

Cinnabar flew out the door just a moment before the hunt went galloping by.

"Yer quarry goes thataway," bawled the miller. "Aye, General, thataway!" And he pointed a bony finger in Cinnabar's direction.

Chapter 10

WHOOOO, YOU?

Cinnabar streaked along the road, letting the breeze of his own making dry his coat. All the mint scent was gone now, and his own foxy fragrance drifted enticingly along behind him.

It spurred the hounds to renewed action, but even so, they couldn't catch him, for the cooling stream had given him new energy. That last little squeaking rat, however, had reminded him of two things. He was hungry; he was famished! And second, had he not made a promise to Vicky? His own words came rushing back at him: "You get the currant jelly. I'll fetch the hen." Somehow I'll do it! he promised himself.

He planned his route as he sped along well ahead of the hunt. "I'll run on down the road a piece, make a big swing through the woods, and by that time I'll be far from those blood-hungry hounds. Then on to Mister Plunkett's henyard, where I'll pick off the best."

His mind was so purposeful now that the sights of the road went unnoticed. He ran past cabins with smoke curling from their chimneys, past a schoolhouse where a forlorn boy was sweeping the steps. He overtook a pair of drowsy mules drawing a great load of tobacco. Farther on, as the road cut through the big woods, a dust cloud came hulking toward him. When the shape of it fell apart, it turned out to be a coach-and-four rattling along at a merry clip. The driver up in his box leaned out as they met. "Yoiks!" he cried to the oncoming hunt. "There goes yer fox! Tally ho!"

A spidery man ran out of a barn, tried to lay hold of Cinnabar's tail, but he slithered out of reach, swerved off the road, and whisked into the dark woods.

The hounds were going so fast they overran the scent and dashed on.

Cinnabar sighed in pure delight at how neatly his plans were working. In the ghostly stillness of the forest,

his padded feet made no noise at all. A gray squirrel chippered at him from the stump of a tree and dropped a beechnut at his feet.

"Hi, nutcracker," Cinnabar called out. "How's the burying business?"

He expected no answer and got none. His mind settled down to his own business at once. "I've baffled the hounds," he grinned in satisfaction. "Now I'll circle through the woods, and so to Mister Plunkett's."

He was making fine progress when the richest,

strongest scent came wafting his way. He took a deep breath and froze in his tracks with wonder and joy. What was this rank, sweet, reasty smell that set his saliva juices working? It made his whole body quiver in excitement. "Why, 'tis fish!" he drooled. "Nice and old and oily! Who has left fish in the forest? Who?"

Deep in a pine tree a ruffled screech owl echoed his thoughts. "Who? Who? Whoooooo?"

Cinnabar paid no heed to the owl. The fulsome fragrance of fish was a magnet pulling him on until suddenly he burst upon the source of the smell. It was a trap, and upon its pan lay a rich chunk of catfish with all of the oily skin left on. As if this were not tempting enough, a sliver of chicken breast was impaled alongside the fish.

"By the great horned spoon!" cried Cinnabar. "And me whose belly is pinched with hunger!" His eyes glanced all around to make sure that no thief was after his prize. He ventured a step closer, and another. Traps held no terror for him. Often and often he had devoured the bait without so much as a hair being caught. "I can do it again!" he exclaimed.

His heart thumping fast, he reached for the inviting morsels, and as his mouth opened to snatch the bait, his left forefoot barely grazed the trigger.

Crack!

All in a shocked instant the iron jaws snapped shut. One of Cinnabar's toes was caught fast! In a panic he tried to jerk free, but the jaws were merciless.

A little cry escaped him. His whole body crumpled. He tried to straighten, tried to shake his foot, but the weight of the trap was almost beyond bearing. He began panting and shivering violently, and his body felt hot and cold at the same time.

He looked about helplessly—helpless against the awful stillness of the forest, and he began a pleading chant. "Oh, let me see them again," and his breath whispered the names over and over, "Rascal, Pascal, Merry, and Mischief; and oh, Vicky, Vicky, Vicky!"

A doe wandered near, studied him with her sad wet eyes. Then quietly she turned tail and left him to his loneliness.

The same brown owl came soundlessly sifting

through the gloom. It swept into a bush over Cinnabar's head, staring blindly with its glassy eyes. "Whoooo? *You?*" it screeched. "Whoooo? *You?*"

Cinnabar hated the owl with a mounting fury. He mustered a pitiful bark, then set to work frantically to tear himself free. He put one forepaw on the trap to steady it, and pulled with all his might. A knife-edge of pain shot up his leg. For a long moment he was too sick to try again.

Up in the sky a crow spied the trapped fox and circled about him. "Caw! Caw!" it screamed raucously, as if enjoying Cinnabar's fate. Then it wheeled away and soon more crows came, a whole flock of croaking, flapping crows, beating their ebony wings in his face. "Caw! Caw! Caw-aw-aw-aw!" they cackled harshly.

All this while the hunt was checked at the edge of the woods. Hounds were catching their breath, horses steaming and blowing, hunters conferring.

"Which way has the One O'Clock Fox gone?"

"To earth?"

"So soon?"

"Surely not! Always before, he has given us a run until dark."

The talk came to a sudden halt as the men heard the racket of the crows.

"Hark!" Billy Lee cried. "Hark to the tattletale birds. They've sighted our fox. Tiy hioui," he called to the hounds. "Leu in! Leu in!"

In his misery Cinnabar sensed what was happening, sensed that he was caught in a double trap. The crows were trapping him, too. His whole body seemed to squeeze together as if it were trying to become invisible. Even his heart felt pinched and little, and hurt.

From the tops of the pine trees more shiny black crows came swooping down, ready to stab him with their bills. The air went wild with their cawing, and now wilder still with the hounds' baying.

There was no time to think. Only time to act. With a fierce grip Cinnabar's teeth clamped down on the trap

and he tore himself free. In a flash he was gone. He felt
no pain in his foot now. Only a dead numbness. But
behind in the trap he had left a toe, and behind him as
he ran a spotting of blood showed darkly on the forest
duff.

Chapter 11

CANDLELIGHT AND AN OPEN DOOR

In a blind daze Cinnabar took off. The press of the hounds forced him away from home, but fortunately he stumbled upon a well-beaten path, smooth and kind to his foot. For nearly a mile he paced steadily ahead of the hunt, his legs pumping like some machine. But as the numbness wore off, the blood began throbbing in the torn foot. It throbbed in his head, too, until he dizzied with pain. The way in front of him began to blur and waver; yet the hounds drove him on. Forward and ever forward over the narrow path, running, struggling, foot and leg burning, the wound stinging hotly as the blood dried.

Desperately he needed a moment to rest and pant, but the hounds were hitting the trail too hard. They were gaining at an alarming rate. He had to go on. He limped along on three legs, then whimpering in pain he made himself go on four.

The dampness of late afternoon was settling down, and with the sureness of a wild thing Cinnabar knew that as the day wore on to evening his chances of escape were less. Already the grasses that overran the path were latching on to his scent with their greedy fingers. He tried deliberately to avoid them, to run down the center, holding his tail high as well. But it drooped tiredly and brushed against them.

The hounds now were in full cry. To drown out their baying, Cinnabar began calling again the names of his family:

> *"Rascal, Pascal, Merry, Mischief,*
> *And oh, Vicky, Vicky, Vicky,*
> *Don't forget me; don't forget me."*

As he chanted, the path began to widen out and join up with a road. The pike to Fredericksburg! It was like some miracle-answer to a prayer. Now there were no grasses to steal his scent. The road was red clay, clean and bare, and so the hounds were slowed.

On he went, across a bumpy bridge over Accotink Creek. On and on. It was torture. His lungs ached and his whole body felt a supreme weariness. Then, as in a dream, he saw ahead an opened door and in the darkness within, a candle burning. It was the door to Pohick church! Once before, he had sought refuge there.

How far to that candle?

Two breaths away?

A dozen?

He fixed on the tiny flame as on a beacon, and he moved toward it in a direct savage motion. When at last he reached the stone steps of the church, he had to take them one at a time. Then he staggered inside.

A choking filled his throat. "Glory be!" he whispered in the high-vaulted stillness. "Glory be! I'm saved!"

The pack of hounds kept right on past the door. But as they lost the scent, they soon came back, fanning around the churchyard, questing. When the hunters arrived on the scene, they thought the pack had lost their wits.

"Sweet Lips! June and Jowler! Chanter and Rhapsody!" In great disgust Billy Lee called the hounds to him and cast them down the pike toward Fredericksburg.

Within the church, Cinnabar felt as secure as if he were in his own den. At first he saw no one. No one at all. He heaved a great sigh and lay down to rest.

He had hardly shut his eyes when a thin, whistling sound skirled out of the air. It was so high-pitched that he winced at the pain to his ears. A moment's silence followed. Then more weeping, wailing notes came tumbling down from the organ loft. The sound repelled Cinnabar, but the smell from the loft intrigued him. Unmistakably it was chicken. Fried.

Hopefully, he got to his feet, pattered up the narrow steps, and stood poised on the topmost one.

Directly in front of him, upon the organ bench, he saw a plump-bodied woman holding a chicken leg in one hand and pounding the keys with the other. All at once she became so excited over the spasm of sound she had created that the drumstick slipped from her hand and fell under the bench. As she leaned over to pick it up, a tawny red body snatched it away and dived under the pedals.

The screech that followed was horrible. For the poor woman, not seeing the fox clearly, thought the strange disappearance of her food was a punishment meted out by the Lord. Leaping from the bench, she ran the full length of the loft and hid behind the door of a small closet. "Oh, saints and little sinners," she sobbed hysterically, "I didn't mean to touch the organ. I didn't mean to. I didn't . . . I didn't."

Keeping his eyes and ears open, Cinnabar devoured the chicken like one starved. He tore each shred of meat from the bone and gulped it whole. Then he chewed the gristle at the joint. As he began polishing the bone, the

door of the closet opened a crack and the white-capped head of the charwoman peeped out. Her beady eyes found his own amber ones, and for a long moment the two creatures regarded one another.

It was the woman who broke the silence. She clucked softly and delightedly, like some mother hen. "Here I thought ye were a spook come to affright me fer tryin' out the organ, and all ye be is a pore little wildling."

Cautiously she emerged from her hiding place. "Oh, and ye've hurt yer paw," she whispered, "and yer tongue is all swolled up from thirst."

So as not to frighten her woodland visitor, she moved

now very slowly, yet lightly too in spite of her bulk. Down the steps she tiptoed, and up the aisle to the baptismal fount, which she had been washing.

Cinnabar crept after her at a safe distance, hoping for more chicken.

"Now, li'l red fox," she breathed, "a nice refreshin' drink is what ye need. And 'tis a lucky thing I forgot to put lye ashes in my scrub bucket today. The water's clear and cool, like it just come from the well."

She took a pewter mug from the pulpit and dipped it into the pail. "Reverend Massey ain't a-going to mind a little woodsy person drinkin' outa his mug . . . leastawise, I don't think so. If'n he does," she chuckled, "I'll just up and say right back at him from his own sermon: 'Inasmuch as ye hae done it unto one of the least of these, ye hae done it unto me!'"

With great ceremony she set the mug on the floor and stepped back a goodly distance. There she stood quite motionless, her hands wrapped in her apron.

After a long moment Cinnabar took a step forward and another, hopping on three legs to save the hurt one. At last he reached the mug, but he had time for only a few good laps of water when his ears came up sharply. His whole body tensed as he heard the hunter's horn calling the hounds together. They were coming back!

His mind was in a whirl. "Shall I bolt for the door?" he asked himself. "No! There's not time. I'm cornered. I'll hide here." Dipping his hurt paw in the water, he

looked up at the charwoman with pleading eyes. "You won't tell on me, will you?"

"'Course not," she replied, as if the plea had been spoken.

Now her head, too, bobbed up in alarm, for across the pews she saw a man's figure blocking the doorway. It was the Kennel Huntsman, Billy Lee, holding the reins of his horse. Quickly she whisked off her apron and dropped it over Cinnabar. Then composing her face as best she could, she called out a wavery "G-g-good evening," and then a "Good evening, *s-s-ir*!" as she recognized, beyond the door, the stately form of General Washington.

Billy Lee waved his cap in excitement. "Ma'am," he

shouted, "have you seen our One O'Clock Fox? 'Tis a draggled dog-fox. You seen him, ma'am?"

The charwoman's eyes wandered from floor to ceiling and back again. They caught the pixielike face of Cinnabar peering out at her. "You won't tell on me, will you?" he asked again.

"Oh, I seed him all right!" yelled the charwoman, half running, half stumbling to the door. "He *was* here, like a whiff and a pfsst, but the good Lord knows where he's at by now!" And then she fell into hysteria. "Heaven's angels, oh heaven's angels, how's a body to get her work done? How's a body to . . ."

Chapter 12

FARMER PLUNKETT, HERE I COME!

In that brief moment huddled in the friendly darkness of the old blue apron, the happenings of the day
flashed through Cinnabar's mind. Great sport, yes! But,
he grudgingly admitted to himself, somewhat more than
he had wanted. What a day!

He listened to the beat of hoofs fading, and to the
dying echo of hound voices. "I best be off while the way

is clear!" he said under his breath. He sat up, letting the apron fall about him like a cloak. He felt surprisingly good. His stomach was comfortable with the delicious chicken he had eaten, his thirst was slaked, and the dizziness in his head was gone. Even his foot had stopped bleeding and the pain was no more than a dull ache.

The charwoman sighed in relief as she came back to Cinnabar. She seemed enormously pleased with herself. "No siree!" she chuckled. "I didn't tell on ye, little Bre'r Fox, did I? And now, feller, ye needn't be perlite about staying on. 'Eat and run' has got to be yer motto, I know. So gie me my apron, and be off with ye."

Cinnabar looked into her kindly face. Then he shook free of the apron, and with a swift, gliding movement skirted his way past the baptismal fount, past the pulpit, past the row of box pews, and out into the haze of late afternoon.

Pohick cemetery stood opposite the door, and Cinnabar bounded aloft a tombstone to get his bearings. He searched the land but saw no shadow of movement. So trusting more to his nose than to his eyes, he faced the breeze, letting his delicate nostrils sift it of its many scents. It told him that the hunters had gone on beyond the church in a southwesterly direction.

"Oh, fat green frogs!" he exclaimed in glee. "They're far off my line!"

He perched a moment atop his observation tower and figured his next move. Home would be to the north and east. And on the way he'd cut through the big woods, and through the sheepfold and cattle pen of Farmer Plunkett. Then he'd be there—right in the chickenyard, the old brushy, weedy, ill-kempt yard where cocks and hens picked and pecked. He'd choose the plumpest one of all; then in no time he'd be back in his own den.

He turned to look at his shadow and saw that his ears were very long and several tombstones away. It was growing late! Vicky would soon be in a panic of worry. He

could almost see her tremble and hear her teeth chattering. He must spare her that and not be too long overdue.

Leaping to earth, he hastened out to the road and made a sharp turn, backtracking the way he had come. Before he had gone far, a horse and rider loomed up on the road ahead of him. Were they members of the hunt? Cinnabar stopped in midflight. Dare he go on and overtake them? Or would it be wiser to drop back and melt into the shadows? Boldly he decided to go on, and was much relieved to find that the man was a circuit rider whom he had seen many times, Preacher Clapsaddle by name. Cinnabar fell into a dogtrot beside the horse.

"What is a single plodding horseman," he shrugged, "when I've been eluding thirty galloping hunters!"

The preacher was reading aloud in his best pulpit voice. "Our text today," his words boomed out over the countryside, "be from the Song of Solomon: 'Take us the foxes, the little foxes, that spoil the vines; for our vines have tender grapes.'"

Solemnly he closed and locked his Bible and then looking down spied the jaunty form of Cinnabar. He was so startled he almost fell out of his saddle. A low gasp escaped him. "'Tis an omen!" he cried. "My sermon is writ. It be a concurrence sent from the Lord."

Cinnabar, unmindful of the dramatic role he had just played, turned off the road and with true homing instinct slid into the big woods. He would take the shortest way.

Once he was homeward bound, the compass in his mind gave him no peace. Its needle pricked and urged him forward. Straight through the woods he traveled. As he ambled along, his ears were tuned to catch the slightest sound. A twig snapped; he froze into a statue. Then he chuckled to himself, for it was only a lazy black bear—fat, full, and heavily furred, ready to hibernate. Farther on, a doe with her nearly grown fawn stomped the ground menacingly, as if Cinnabar had no right to her woods.

"So be you!" he barked curtly. This was Grandma Bushy's favorite way of ending any argument.

Suddenly the peace of the woods shattered. To the right of him Cinnabar heard the hounds yapping, and ahead he smelled man-smell. He hated this man-smell with an especial hate, for it was Farmer Grimm's. Stooped over like a jackknife, the man was laughing harshly to himself as he baited another of his vicious traps. A crick in his back caused him to straighten up with a start.

Rubbing the sore muscle, he let his eyes rove, and all in the same instant he saw Cinnabar and heard the hunters. A fiendish grin crossed his face. Cupping his hands to his mouth, he bellowed his find to the oncoming hunt. "Here's yer varmint! Here he be!"

Like some great scudding cloud the cavalcade swept through the woods in Cinnabar's direction.

Cinnabar was off! Through the big trees, weaving around tree trunks, leaping fallen logs, then through sumac and hawthorn and out onto a brown meadow. There were no paths to follow, only paths to make— in the tall grass, over tussocks and hummocks, over the tangled matting of many years. And now the wiry blades cut the pads of his feet until the torn place began to sting again.

He made spy hops by leaping high above the grass. How far had he come? Was it a hundred yards to Farmer Plunkett's? Two hundred yards?

A sheep blatted as if in answer. Why, he was practically there! He *was* there! The stone-and-rail fence was just ahead. With a magnificent bound he reached the

top rail and went teetering along like a man on a tight-rope. The hounds were close on him now, frenzied by the nearness, their voices sharper and shriller for the kill.

But inside the penfold the whole flock of sheep seemed in league with Cinnabar. Mouths open, heels kicking dust, they jammed close to the rails, baa-aaing and blatting as if their lives, too, were at stake. As Sweet Lips jumped at the fence, Cinnabar's body made a flying arc into the air. He landed on the soft, woolly back of a great ewe in the very center of the flock.

"Whee, and oh whee!" he cried, treading the billowing gray wave of sheep, vaulting from one to another, nipping at their necks to drive them forward. Like a bareback rider in a circus he rode the sheep across the field until the view-halloo of the hunters gave way to cheers of amazement and admiration.

Again they were outfoxed! To head him off they had to gallop all the way around two enclosures, one for the sheep and one for the cattle. The hounds, too, were baffled, for all of the precious fox scent was mingled and lost among the sheep.

Cinnabar's voice trilled in mischievous enjoyment. "Oh, what sport! This day was worth waiting for." And as he jumped from back to back, he sang an old nursery rhyme he had taught his youngsters:

> *"O, a hunter went a-hunting, O,*
> *And he wished to leap a gate.*
> *Said the owner, 'Go around*
> *With your horse and your hound,*
> *For never shall you leap my gate.'*

Ha, ha, ha! Ho, ho, ho! And here I come, Mister Plunkett, ready or not!"

Leaping to the ground, he rushed headlong through the penfold, gained the top rail of the fence on the far side, and dived into the pasture where the excited cows were hightailing it from fence to fence.

Farmer Plunkett, musket in hand, now came running, not toward Cinnabar but toward the cow pasture. "Stop!" he yelled to the hunters, failing to recognize General Washington. "You're worritin' my cows and they'll gie me no milk. Stop, I tell ye!" And he waved his musket high, his trigger finger curved.

Cinnabar forced himself to look away from the fun. Then he squeezed under the bottom rail of the cattle pen and into the henyard where the silly chickens froze to earth as they heard the wild confusion.

"There is no time to lose," Cinnabar panted. "While the farmer scolds the hunters, I'll pick off Vicky's plump hen, and then home!"

Chapter 13

MUSKET FIRE

It was exactly as Vicky had said. Farmer Plunkett's henyard was in a sorry condition. Not only was the fence in a higgledy-piggledy state, but the yard itself was a scraggle of brush and weeds.

Thinking now of his promise to Vicky, Cinnabar slithered his way deeper into the henyard. He would select the choicest bird in the flock and carry it off in spite of his pursuers!

The sun was dipping down behind the far hills, but

before it slid from sight it picked out a hen in a setting mood. She had built her nest in a hideaway place, but the last long sun-shafts found her. Cinnabar considered a moment as she regarded him with her red-rimmed eyes. Then his mind pulled away from the thought. "No!" he decided. "I will *not* snatch her up. Where's the sport in taking a setting hen? I *will* not do it! And besides," he reminded himself, "setting hens are poor pickin's. Vicky wants her birds young and juicy."

Moving stealthily, he inched his way to the center of the yard and crouched there quite concealed among the weeds. He had not long to wait. As horses and hounds neared, the hypnotized chickens suddenly came alive and a whole running parade streamed right at Cinnabar. They were led by a gay-feathered, high-stepping cockerel who pumped along at a jerky one-two gait.

"*He's* my bird!" Cinnabar whispered joyfully. "Young and fleshy, and too cocky for his own good."

And just when Cinnabar was up on his toes, ready for the pounce, a musket ball whistled by his ear. It was close, close as a hair. Where it hit, Cinnabar had no idea. All he knew was that the whole yard became a whirlwind of fluttering, squawking chickens. With perfect timing, he sprang into the melee, grabbed the cockerel in mid-air, and bolted out of the yard, in full view of a groom riding toward the hunt. The groom, who had been trying to catch up, was leading a fresh pair of horses for the general and Billy Lee. The horses were so eager to

join the chase that Cinnabar took a great risk in dashing between their nervous feet.

"Thar he goes!" cried the groom as the fleeing Cinnabar narrowly escaped a second round of musket fire.

Cinnabar was puzzled as he ran. The bird in his mouth was not flapping and struggling, but hung limp and quiet. He did not know that the shot intended for him had instantly killed the cock.

His day almost complete, Cinnabar thought he had never been so happy. He was homeward bound. His heart was full of home! And in his mouth, the nice prize for Vicky and the pups. What if musket shot whirred and whined around his head? It couldn't stop him. Nothing could!

He flew in and out among the farm buildings—past the wagon shed, the woodshed, the washhouse, past the smokehouse and the pigsty. There was danger in coming this way, but it was quicker and it would slow the hounds. As he cut around the farmhouse, he planned his course carefully. He would head for the North Branch of Dogue Run, float downstream to his own woods, and then he'd be only a hoot and a holler from home.

He looked back and saw the general hastily changing horses. Even with his mouth full of feathers, Cinnabar managed a throaty chuckle. He had worn out the General's mount, and now he was losing the farmer in his very own farmyard! Mister Plunkett had stumbled over a tree root, discharged his musket, and scattered the hounds galley-west!

For nearly a half mile Cinnabar trotted a straight-away line for the creek. It was an easy downhill course, easy underfoot, with few ridgy places to hurt his torn pad. But as he tired from his burden, it seemed farther than he had thought. At times he went knee-deep in grass, with milkweed pods waving above his head and late asters nodding. And the longer he traveled, the heavier the bird seemed—for it was dead weight, fully one-third of his own. It pulled his head down, and a tiredness began washing over him like a wave. Only a little while ago he had been full of chuckles. Now he felt small, and burdened, and alone under a vast sky.

The evening wind blew up to him from the creek. He clenched his jaws tighter on the cock. "Cinny!" He

tried to make believe Vicky was calling to him. "Cinny, it is only a little piece farther to the creek. You can make it, Cinny! You can make it. I know you can."

The yipping cries of Sweet Lips and the hounds broke into his thoughts. He looked back again and saw the grasses swaying, and he knew that the pack was pressing hard.

He made his legs go. The good foot, the hurt foot, hind left with front right, hind right with front left. A little more, and a little more. "I believe in you, Cinnabar. Trot! Trot! Trot faster! Faster!"

Only seconds ahead of the hounds he reached the swift-flowing creek. Here it was—his old friend, the creek—rippling and laughing up at him.

He slipped into its cool wetness, tightening his hold on the cock as if it might come alive and fly away. He looked over his shoulder, measuring his distance from the hounds, and then he looked ahead to home. He could still make it! He turned over now, letting the current cradle him. It carried him surely, steadily. Yet how gentle it was! How very gentle! He looked up at the dusky heavens. A few stars winked at him. He guessed he knew now how it must feel to be a cloud, a little cloud floating in a deep sky.

He held the cock with his forepaws and just drifted along as the busy creek flowed on to meet the river. Wearily he closed his eyes, enjoying a moment of restfulness. His bushy tail lay floating stilly upon the water,

so that when the hunters were close enough to sight him, they wondered, "Can he . . . can he be *dead*?"

As if in reply, Cinnabar wheeled around, snatched the cock in his teeth again, and swam strongly to the far bank.

His quick movements set off a whole chain of explosions behind him. Hounds plunged into the water and, one by one, thirty horsemen began fording the creek. The very air went wild with noise. Men's cries mingled with the screaming of hounds and the plash of hoofs. It was like thunder crashing nearer and nearer.

Quick, Cinnabar! Across the meadow and into your woods! Quick! Into the woods for your life! Now legs pumping, lungs pumping. Go. Go. Go. The air burned his nose as he sucked it in. The cock grew heavier and heavier and its spindly legs seemed to grow longer and longer. They flapped against him, getting in his way so that his gait lost its rhythm.

Behind him, the whirl of hounds whipped closer and closer. They were hammering his trail with a fierce joy. They would catch him, unless . . . ? The question spun in his mind. Drop the cockerel? Drop it?

No! No! Run, run, run! You might make it.

Earth coming at him. Woods coming at him. Big pines making way for him. This way, Cinnabar, this way. The trees must be moving! The whole forest streamed past him, so fast was his pace. His lungs seemed on fire, but he was going to make it! From his game heart he drew the last ounce of strength. In one breathless spurt he reached the old familiar sassafras thicket. And then—oh praises be!—he was almost drawn inside his den by the curling fingers of his own clump of ferns. As

in a dream he heard the voice of George Washington rocketing through the woods: "The One O'Clock Fox is going to earth. Call off your hounds, Billy Lee; 'twas a magnificent run!"

With a gay swish of his brush, Cinnabar disappeared into the black hollow of his den. More plainly than any words it said: "Thank you, one and all! Thank *you*, Sweet Lips, and *you*, General Washington, and all you hounds and gentlemen!"

Then dropping the cock he spun around and poked his elfin face out of the earth.

"I had jolly fun, too!" he barked to the hunters. Then he frisked his black whiskers, gave them all a wide grin, and was gone.

Chapter 14

LIFE IS NICE AND ROUND

Gloriously happy, his tiredness forgotten, Cinnabar went wriggling down the passageway to his family. He noticed that the cockerel's feathers were the worse for being dragged through bog and briar and meadow and mire, but he knew his Vicky would still consider it a fine fowl. That was one reason he prized her so much; she saw beneath feathers and fur, and . . .

Cinnabar had no time to finish his thought, for Rascal, Pascal, Merry, and Mischief were waiting for him and now sprang, leaping upon him, rolling him over, biting his big peaked ears, bouncing about him like kittens.

"Oh me, oh me!" Cinnabar laughed indulgently. "I might better have been mauled by the hounds!"

In a high state of glee, Rascal now snatched up the cock and raced around and around the table, while Pascal and Merry and Mischief ran after him. A great mock battle arose with Mischief tearing harmlessly at Rascal's furry throat and Merry biting his brush.

"Children!" Vicky entreated. "Your father needs peace and quiet. Stop chasing about and hush up. Please!"

But there was so much growling and yapping that her voice was lost. In desperation, she took the twin flute from its lovely case and blew a single high note.

The effect was electric. Each cub froze into position. They became a little audience of four, quietly watching, listening for what might come.

The stillness was complete as Vicky nosed the tattered feathers of the cockerel and bunted it over with keen appraisal. Then her delicate forepaws fluttered in pleasure. "Oh, what a beautiful, lovely, delectable, plump bird! My currant jelly is hardly worthy of it. But, Cinny, however did you manage to snatch a cockerel? They are so much harder to take than the hens. How *ever* did you *do* it?"

Up on his hind feet, Cinnabar leaned against the fireplace, one elbow on the mantel. He cleared his throat, and

his voice was deep and hearty. "It was nothing. Nothing at all. I was glad to do it for you. Next time I'll bring you a suckling pig, or perhaps even a lamb," he chuckled. "I had so much fun getting it for you. If it delights you, I am happy."

"But how *did* you get it? How did you *do* it?"

"If the truth must be known, my dear, 'twas the good gift of Providence, aided and abetted by your Mister Plunkett. He was most obliging."

"In the matter of poor fences?"

"Oh, more! Much, much more! Just as I was leaping for the cock, a shot intended for me must have hit him. He jumped high in the air, where I caught him."

Aghast at this narrow escape, Vicky quite suddenly crumpled to the floor in a dead faint. It took two gourdsful of water thrown hastily in her face to bring her back to consciousness. Embarrassed, she was soon on her feet, vigorously wiping her face with her apron. Then she examined Cinnabar from the black tip of his ears to the white tip of his brush. When she had made certain that he was all of one piece, she gave a great sigh of thankfulness. Somehow the matter of the lost toe on his left forepaw completely escaped her—perhaps because Cinnabar showed her his right forepaw twice. Now she turned to the spellbound pups.

"Children," she said, and her face became solemn, "this bird is the good gift of Providence. So your father says. But oh, how he helps Providence!" Her voice now became as serious as her face. "Your papa," she proclaimed, "is the greatest hunter I ever knew in all my life. He's the greatest hunter in the whole wide world. The greatest! And now," she sighed, "before we pluck the bird clean, I want you all to wait upon your papa in the way that he deserves." Then she clipped out directions:

"Rascal! You fetch the goose grease and melt it in the warming oven.

"Pascal! You fetch your father's comb, and comb the mud from his coat.

115

"Merry! You pour your father a spot of dandelion juice.

"Mischief! You hang a pot of water over the fire."

Cinnabar had to laugh to himself. Families are wonderful, he thought. They make you out a hero when all you have done is to snatch a bird in midair.

With only a slight limp, he went over to Grandma Bushy's rocker and eased his bones into its welcoming arms. He let everyone wait upon him because it was giving *them* so much fun. The dandelion juice soothed his gullet as Pascal combed the mud from his brush, and Vicky worked on the pads of his feet with the goose grease. When she came to the left forepaw, she began silently to weep as if the missing toe were more her loss than his own.

"Oh, come now, Vicky! Who's to miss a toe? Not I! Not I! Besides, it sent me into a very fine church, where . . ."

"Where you probably hid rather than repented!" Vicky laughed through her tears.

"That's my girl!" Cinnabar patted her head. Suddenly he yowled in mock pain. "Your tears are dreadful salty on my wound, Vicky. Please to shut them off at once."

When Cinnabar was made very comfortable, he lolled back in the rocker, his paws folded across his chest. "Let come the blizzard," he barked softly. "Let come the blizzard—of feathers."

The children looked with asking eyes from Cinnabar to the cockerel to their mother, who now sang out: "Get ready! Get set! Pluck!"

In a flashing instant four furry bodies pounced on the cockerel and began plucking feathers until the den was a rousing, rollicking storm with shooting geysers of white whenever anyone sneezed. In no time at all the bird was plucked clean, except for a few pinfeathers.

"*I* shall cut it up," announced Vicky, "for even though your father appears fresh as a daisy, he must be bone weary."

"I want a wing!" shouted Merry.

"Me, too!" shouted Mischief.

"I want a drumstick!" This was Pascal's voice, quite deep for his age.

"Me, too!" echoed Rascal. "Me, too."

By now the pot was boiling. "The water has stopped

smiling; it's laughing out loud!" Mischief announced as she looked into the steaming pot.

Vicky dropped the pieces into the bubbling water. Then she turned the tiny three-minute glass that stood on the mantel. "'Tis lucky," she said to Cinnabar, "that we are only six. For you and I can split the back and breast; and that is all there is."

Now everyone gathered about the table, letting their eyes wander over the bowls of beetles and crickets and sauces and seasonings. But mostly they fixed upon the bright red mounds of quivering currant jelly. Everyone helped himself, while Vicky ladled out the steaming pieces of chicken in giblet broth. And so the meal began!

It was impossible to eat without making noises—loud crunching noises and soft slurping ones.

Cinnabar rubbed his stomach and smacked his lips. "It's delicious!" he said. "Nice and rare!"

"It's yummy," the children barked.

"'Tis a prime fowl," agreed Vicky.

A good feeling came over everyone. Cinnabar looked on his family in great satisfaction. And when he had done with his chicken breast, he fell asleep right at the table, holding the wishbone in his hurt paw.

"Sh!" whispered Vicky. "Let the poor dear sleep. He's had such a hard day."

"Sh!"

"Sh!"

"Sh!"

"Sh!" echoed the four children, but their shushes were so loud that Cinnabar awoke with a jerk. The forty winks of sleep had greatly refreshed him, however.

He went back to Grandma Bushy's rocker and motioned to the cubs to follow. They sat down at his feet, curling their tails neatly about them.

"Please, Papa," they begged, "tell us about the hunt."

Pulling at his whiskers and clearing his throat to heighten the suspense, Cinnabar sat back and began to brag in a nice kind of way. "Oh, I gave them a first-rate gallop," he chuckled. "And if *my* paws are cut and torn, you should see the hounds' ears! Oh, everyone had a capital time. I muddied their coats, lamed their horses and hounds, but they never caught me! Not on your lefe, lofe, life!" He drummed his toes in remembrance. "Right at the first I gave them a tremendous run!"

"Where?"

"Where?"

"Where?"

"Where?"

"In the new green wheatfield, down on Union Farm."

"Then what?"

"I baffled them."

"How, Papa?"

"I ran them in circles until I was chasing *them*. Ho, ho!"

"How else, Papa?"

"I foiled my scent in pennyroyal mint."

"How else?"

"I rode on the backs of sheep!"

"How else?"

"I floated downstream in Dogue Run."

"And how did the Master of the Foxhounds do?" This was Vicky's question.

"Oh, creditably, my dear. Quite creditably. The general tried hard to outwit me. He leaped logs and went fairly fast without standing up in his stirrups. He didn't catch me, but my guess is he caught the ague. Ho, ho, ho! And all his horses were beat! Completely done up! The fact is, my dear, I set the pace so fast that the general couldn't change horses until I was busy at Farmer Plunkett's!"

"Children," Vicky's eyes shone with pride, "see how the whole countryside must respect your father. In years to come, when you hear tales of the One O'Clock Fox, hold your heads high, my dears, for it is of your father's skill and gallantry that they speak. And now," she added, turning to Cinnabar, "would not this be a good moment to give words of advice? For soon it will be clicketing time, and our children will set up dens of their own."

"What's clicketing time, Mamma?" asked Pascal.

"'Tis mating time, my son."

"Aye," nodded Cinnabar. "Soon you will all be finding dens of your own."

"Oh, *no!*" cried Mischief in alarm.

"*Oh*, no!" wailed Merry.

"Will we!" exclaimed Rascal in great interest.

"Will we?" asked Pascal.

"That you will," said Cinnabar. "But always, in time of danger, this den will be your sure refuge.

"Life is nice and round," he continued reflectively. "No beginning. No ending. I am now arrived at an age when you, my children, will carry on for me. Hand me that looking glass, my dear."

Vicky gave Cinnabar the glass, and he held it up to catch his reflection. "Yes, I must admit to a few white whiskers among the black. I don't doubt but that I am one of the few foxes at Mount Vernon ever to reach my ripe age. And why?" he prompted.

"Why, Papa?"

"Why?"

"Why?"

"Why?"

"Because I have learned that man is a kindly animal with some affection for wild creatures, but you can never trust him completely. The moment you do, it may cost you your life."

With this word of advice, Cinnabar snored a few snores, while the children, at their mother's request, jumped to their feet and stood in line, one behind the other. Their eyes twinkled in expectancy.

"What's this? What's this?" Cinnabar asked upon awakening.

Vicky grinned almost shyly. Then she went over to his rocker and sat down upon the arm of it. "While you were gone on the hunt today," she began, "I told the children about the little ditty you used to sing to *me*. I told them that there was a couplet for each of them."

"A *couplet*?" Cinnabar repeated, scratching his ear.

"Aye, a couplet."

"What's that, Vicky?"

"Oh, Cinny, you know. 'Tis two lines of a poem. Remember the one about the four little foxes?"

Cinnabar's face lighted as he thought of the rhyme. He lifted Merry by her forepaws and dandled her on his knee. Then in a voice full of chuckles he began the rollicking rhythm:

"Four little fox cubs, out upon a spree;
One found a rabbit trap. Then there were three!

"Come, Rascal, 'tis your turn:

"Three little fox cubs, nothing much to do,
Met up with foxhounds. Then there were two!

"Come, Pascal, 'tis your turn:

"Two little fox cubs saw a great big gun.
A man was behind it. Then there was one!

"Come, Mischief, 'tis your turn:

"One little fox cub, coy and full of tricks,
Met a little dog-fox. Now there are six!"

Again and again Cinnabar had to dandle each pup upon his knee until he sank back in exhaustion. And at last the den settled down to quiet, while across the vast of night came the lonely baying of a lost hound still on the scent.

Cinnabar smiled and sighed in consummate bliss. "Life is nice and round," he mumbled happily. "Nice and round."

For their help the author is grateful to

GEORGE WOOD, Joint M.F.H., Wayne DuPage Hunt,
    Wayne, Illinois
WILLIAM WINQUIST, Huntsman, Wayne, Illinois
TERESA ANTONINI, Hollywood Public Library,
    Hollywood, Florida
WILLIAM HARRISON BARNES, authority on old organs,
    Evanston, Illinois
R. GORDON HINNERS, JR., vocalist, St. Charles, Illinois
MARY ALICE JONES, Methodist Board of Education,
    Nashville
MILDRED G. LATHROP, Reference Librarian, Elgin, Illinois
PEGGY RYDER, Hollywood Public Library, Hollywood,
    Florida
ROBERTA B. SUTTON, Reference Librarian, Chicago Public
    Library
EUGENIA WHELAN, Librarian, Hollywood Public Library,
    Hollywood, Florida
IDA G. WILSON, Librarian, Elgin, Illinois
MR. AND MRS. W. R. BEAN, Hollywood, Florida
MR. AND MRS. F. K. BREITHAUPT, Hollywood, Florida
DR. AND MRS. G. H. FELLMAN, Milwaukee, Wisconsin
AVIS GRANT SWICK, St. Charles, Illinois

and especially to
Dorothy Dennis